THOMAS THE TANK ENGINE & FRIENDS

™

ANNUAL 1999

Britt Allcroft's Thomas the Tank Engine & Friends
Based on The Railway Series by The Rev W Awdry.

© Britt Allcroft (Thomas) Limited, 1998.

THOMAS THE TANK ENGINE & FRIENDS is a
trademark of Britt Allcroft Inc in the USA, Mexico
and Canada and of Britt Allcroft (Thomas) Limited in the rest of the world.

All publishing and underlying copyright worldwide WH Books Limited.

The BRITT ALLCROFT COMPANY logo is a trademark
of The Britt Allcroft Company plc.

Published in Great Britain in 1998 by World International Limited,
Deanway Technology Centre, Wilmslow Road, Handforth, Cheshire, SK9 3FB.

Printed in Italy ISBN 0 7489 3764 0

CONTENTS

A Message from Thomas 5
Blooming Railways 8
Read with Thomas 14
Famous Engines 16
Can You Remember? 20
Which Way? 21
Bill and Ben 22
Double Trouble 26
Twins 27
Ten Trucks 28
Make a Thomas Bookmark 30
Leaves on the Line 32
Puffing Engines 36
Competition 38
A Very Busy Day 40
Steam Power 44
Percy's Puzzle 45
Toby Saves the Day 46
Read with Thomas 52
Count with Thomas 53
Thomas Around the World 54
Blowing Bubbles 56
Bubbles 60
Answers to Puzzles 61

A Message from Thomas

Hello, everyone!

I'm **Thomas the Tank Engine**. Welcome to my new book. As you know, I live and work on the railway on the Island of Sodor. I'm very proud to be the Number 1 engine. I work hard on my own branch line with my coaches Annie and Clarabel, who were given to me as a reward for being a Really Useful Engine. Annie carries passengers and Clarabel carries luggage as well as passengers.

I share a shed near the yard with five of my engine friends. I'll tell you all about them.

Edward the Blue Engine is Number 2.

He's an older engine and he's very kind to everyone, small engines like me as well as big engines like Gordon.

Henry the Green Engine is Number 3.

He's very proud of his shiny green paint and is a very fast, smart-looking engine.

5

Gordon the Big Express Engine is Number 4.

He's the senior engine, and makes sure we other engines don't forget it! But he's kind, too, and is always ready to help get us out of trouble.

James the Red Engine is Number 5.

He thinks he's a Really Splendid Engine because of his smart red paint and his shiny brass dome.

Percy the Small Engine is Number 6.

He's the smallest engine, and the youngest. Percy is not very adventurous, and is never happier than when he's working in the yard with the trucks.

6

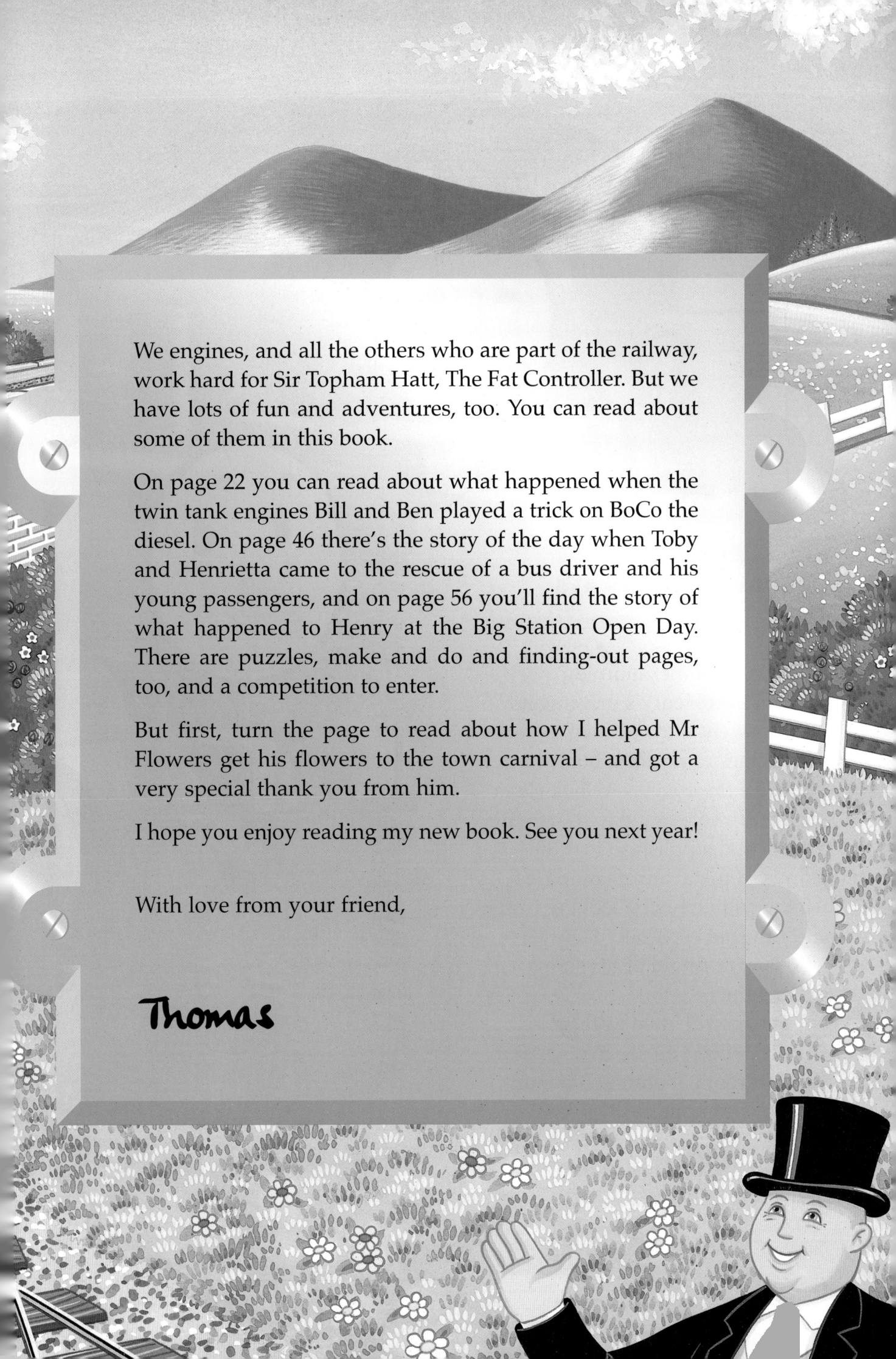

We engines, and all the others who are part of the railway, work hard for Sir Topham Hatt, The Fat Controller. But we have lots of fun and adventures, too. You can read about some of them in this book.

On page 22 you can read about what happened when the twin tank engines Bill and Ben played a trick on BoCo the diesel. On page 46 there's the story of the day when Toby and Henrietta came to the rescue of a bus driver and his young passengers, and on page 56 you'll find the story of what happened to Henry at the Big Station Open Day. There are puzzles, make and do and finding-out pages, too, and a competition to enter.

But first, turn the page to read about how I helped Mr Flowers get his flowers to the town carnival – and got a very special thank you from him.

I hope you enjoy reading my new book. See you next year!

With love from your friend,

Thomas

Blooming Railways

Early one summer morning Thomas and Henry's drivers and firemen went into the shed to get the engines ready for a busy day. They like the engines to look clean and smart, so every day starts with a wash and a polish so that the paint and metal are gleaming. All the engines enjoy looking neat and tidy, but especially Henry, who is very proud of his shiny green paint.

The men chatted as they worked. "Did you see the poster in the staff room about the Blooming Railways competition?" asked Thomas' driver.

"No," said Henry's driver. "What's it all about?"

Thomas' driver explained. "It's a contest that any railway can enter. There's a special prize for the railway that has the best display of flowers."

"It sounds interesting," said Henry's fireman. "Do you think we'll be able to enter?"

"It would be good to try," said Thomas' driver. "But we'd need an awful lot of flowers and plants, and I don't know where we'd get them from. They would cost a lot of money."

"Let's think about it," said Thomas' fireman. "We'll talk to the others later."

Later that morning, Thomas and his driver were working on the quarry branch line as usual. They had taken all the people to work and were heading back when Thomas saw a man standing by the side of the line waving at him.

"Peep, peep!" said Thomas, to let his driver know that something was happening up ahead.

9

When Thomas' driver saw the man waving at him to stop, he put on the brakes. He knew the man. It was Bob Flowers, who has a nursery near the railway where he grows plants and flowers. "What's wrong, Bob?" asked Thomas' driver.

"Thanks for stopping," said Bob. "I'm very glad to see you!" He pointed to the flower fields and greenhouses at the nursery. "I've been growing flowers to decorate the floats that are taking part in the town carnival this afternoon. I'm entering a float of my own, too. I've got boxes and boxes of flowers that I was going to drive into town, but my truck has broken down. Can you help, do you think?"

"Of course we can!" said Thomas' driver. "We don't have to be back for a while."

Thomas agreed. "Peep, peep!" he said.

Soon Mr Flowers and his wife were loading boxes of flowers on to Thomas' coaches, Annie and Clarabel. They were more used to carrying passengers, but they liked having the flowers on board because they smelled so nice.

"The floats are all waiting near the bus station in town," said Mr Flowers. "They'll be decorated there, then set off down the High Street. But Thomas won't be able to take them all the way, will he? How will we get the flowers from the station to the bus depot?"

Thomas' driver had already thought about that. "We'll take you and the flowers to the crossing just this side of the Big Station," he said. "We'll meet Bertie the Bus there, and he can take you into town."

"Brilliant!" said Mr Flowers.

Soon Thomas and his coaches were chuffing along happily. In no time at all they got to the crossing and Mr Flowers and his wife loaded the boxes on to Bertie. Thomas and Annie and Clarabel were happy to have helped. "Peep, peep!" said Thomas as Bertie drove off. "Good luck!"

Bertie got Mr and Mrs Flowers to the bus station in good time to deliver the flowers and decorate their float. The carnival parade set off on time, and was a great success. Lots of people lined the street to watch.

The next day when Thomas was chugging back from the quarry he saw Mr Flowers standing by the side of the line again. And again Mr Flowers waved at Thomas.

Thomas' driver put on the brakes and Thomas stopped.

"Look at this!" said Mr Flowers. "We won first prize in the carnival parade for our flower float. We've got our photograph on the front page of the newspaper! And it's all thanks to you and Thomas and Bertie. We couldn't have done it without you."

Thomas' driver read the newspaper report. "Well done!" he said. "We were happy to help." Then he looked at his watch. "Sorry, but we've got to be going now. We want to enter the Blooming Railways contest and we're having a meeting to decide if we can manage it. We'll have to raise lots of money to buy seeds and bulbs."

Mr Flowers handed Thomas' driver two big sacks. "No need!" he said. "These sacks are full of flower seeds and bulbs. It's my way of saying thank you for your help."

"That's great!" said Thomas' driver. "Just what we need! Thanks, Bob!" The railway staff were soon busy with spades and trowels, planting flowerbeds, window boxes and hanging baskets. They kept them watered, and soon green shoots started to appear. Soon the station and the flowerbeds along the side of the railway line were ablaze with flowers of all shapes, sizes and colours. Thomas liked the forget-me-nots best, because they were blue, just like him.

12

One day a judge from the Blooming Railways competition came to look at the flowers and decide which railway had the best display. The engines were decorated for the big day. They all wore garlands of flowers around their funnels.

The engines and their drivers could hardly wait to hear the result.

They all held their breath when the announcement was made, even Sir Topham Hatt, The Fat Controller. "I am very pleased to announce that your railway has won FIRST PRIZE!" said the judge. "Well done!"

Sir Topham Hatt stepped forward to collect the big silver cup that was the special prize. He knew that Mr Flowers had given the drivers the flower seeds and bulbs as a way of saying thank you for Thomas' help. "Well done, Thomas!" he said. "Well done, everyone!"

Thomas felt very pleased and proud. "Peep, peep!" he said. "Blooming marvellous!"

Read with Thomas

"Read this story yourself.

There are little pictures in place of some words, to help you."

One day the [picture] went to see the engines.

It was a very windy day. The wind blew the Station Master's [picture] away!

[picture] found the flag for the [picture]. It was on his [picture].

The [picture] blew Sir Topham Hatt's [picture] away!

"Peep, peep!" said [picture]. "Where can it be?"

The [picture] looked for the hat.

They looked on the [picture].

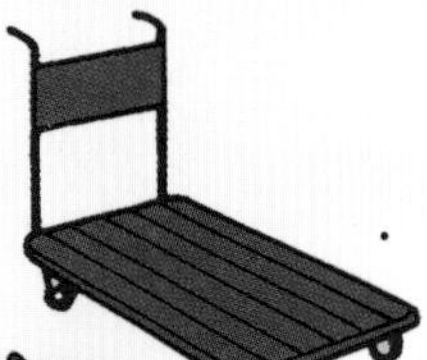

They looked in the [picture].

They looked in the [picture].

They looked in the

They looked in the

They looked in the

They even looked behind the big station

"Where can the hat be?" said   . He went to ask if Gordon had seen it.

          had some dust in his boiler. It made him sneeze.

Atishoo! Out of Gordon's   came Sir Topham's Hatt's hat!

"The wind blew it down your funnel!" said

"Hello. My name is Gordon, engine number 4. I'm the senior member of the engine family. I'm the fastest and most powerful of Sir Topham Hatt's engines and I always do the important job of pulling the big Express train. I'm quite a famous engine, and on these pages I'm going to tell you about some other VERY famous engines."

Locomotion was the name of the first locomotive engine to pull a passenger train. It ran on the first public railway line, which took people between Stockton and Darlington in the north of England.

Locomotion was built by an engineer called George Stephenson and his son Robert a very long time ago, in 1825. The railway line was built for carriages to be pulled along the rails by horses. But Mr Stephenson believed that his new steam engine could do the job better, and decided to prove it.

George Stephenson not only invented and built Locomotion Number 1. He also drove the engine himself!

The word Locomotion means 'movement from place to place'.

Another railway line was built a few years later, in 1829. It ran between the cities of Liverpool and Manchester. The owners held a contest to find the best kind of engine to run on the line. Three engines entered the contest.

Stockton & Darlington

Liverpool & Manchester

16

Steam engines were a very unusual sight, and caused a lot of excitement. A big crowd of 10,000 people watched the contest. Some of them sat on raised platforms so that they could see better.

Each locomotive had to pull a train that weighed three times as much as itself. They had to make 40 trips along a short piece of track.

The first engine was called **Novelty**. It set off very fast, but did not last long. There was a small explosion and Novelty blew up. It was out of the contest.

An engine called **Sans Pareil** (which is French for 'without equal') was next. It did a few trips and covered about 40 kilometres. But a leak in its boiler meant it was out of the contest, too.

An engine built by George Stephenson was next. It was called **Rocket**, and could travel faster than his first engine, Locomotion. Rocket completed the test. It covered a distance of about 56 kilometres in just under two hours. Rocket proved that steam locomotives could work well, and it became the model for many other engines. Rocket's prize was £500, which was a lot of money nearly 200 years ago!

George Stephenson's "Rocket". A prize winner built in 1829.

America is a very big country. Before railways were built there, the only way that people and goods could move around was by water, on horses or on foot. The railways made getting around over long distances much easier and quicker.

The first locomotive to be tried out on rails in America was called **Stourbridge Lion**. It was built in England and taken across the ocean to America on a big ship. It was used for the first time in 1829.

Mallard was a famous English locomotive engine that held the world record for speed in 1938. It reached a speed of 203 kilometres an hour

Steam locomotives got bigger and bigger. They could travel faster and faster and pull heavier and heavier weights.

The largest steam locomotive of all was built in America in 1941. It was called **Big Boy**, and was one hundred times heavier than Rocket! It carried goods, especially in places where the railway had to climb high mountains.

Stourbridge Lion - Built in England and then shipped to the United States.

Why not look at books in your local or school library to find out more about famous steam engines? You could also visit the National Railway Museum in York and see Mallard and Rocket.

The Mallard - The fastest locomotive in 1938.

Gordon says, "How much do you remember about the famous engines? See if you can answer these questions about them."

1. What was the name of the engine that won a big competition in 1829?

2. Which steam engine's name means 'movement from place to place'?

3. What is the name of the biggest steam locomotive ever built?

"Big Boy", built in 1941, was the largest locomotive ever made.

4. Was Mallard an American or an English engine?

5. What was the name of the first steam engine to run on rails in America?

The answers are on page 61.

Can You Remember?

"Here's a fun game to play. Look hard at the ten things on this page. Now close the book and see how many you can remember. Say each name out loud and count on your fingers. Can you remember all ten? No peeping! Peep, peep!"

FIRE

Which Way?

Edward the Blue engine has a problem. He has to get to the Big Station, but he can't remember which is the best way to get there! Can you help him find the way?

Which is the right track, A, B, C, D, or E?

The answer is on page 61.

E

D

A

B

C

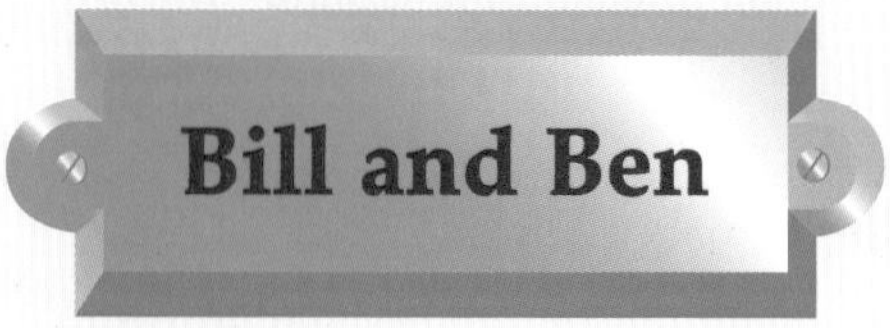

Bill and Ben

1. Bill and Ben are twin tank engines. They are the same colour, and both have four wheels, a tiny chimney and dome, and a small cab.

2. Bill and Ben look alike. The only thing that is different about them is their names!

3. Bill and Ben work between the quarry and Brendam Bay, which is a port on Edward's line. Like most ports, it is a very busy place.

4. Bill and Ben have lots of jobs to do. They pull trucks for ships and boats in the harbour. They also pull engines on the main line.

5. One day Bill and Ben's driver takes off their name plates. He likes them to look smart, so he's going to give them a good polish.

6. Bill and Ben are good friends with BoCo, the big diesel engine. They like teasing him, and decide to play a little trick on him.

7. "Good morning, BoCo," says Bill. "I'd like to stop and chat, but I'm much too busy. I'm taking all these trucks to the Big Station."

8. "Good morning, BoCo," says Ben. "I can't stop and chat to you because I'm very busy. I have to collect some trucks from a ship in the harbour."

9. "Goodbye, BoCo!" says Bill. "Goodbye, BoCo!" says Ben. The twin engines set off very fast. One goes one way and one goes the other way.

10. BoCo is very surprised when the engine he thinks is Bill comes back from the wrong direction, from the harbour! It's very puzzling!

11. BoCo is even more surprised when the engine he thinks is Ben comes back from the Big Station. What is going on?

12. The twin engines don't stop to talk to BoCo. They rush off again, as fast as they can. One goes one way, and one goes the other way.

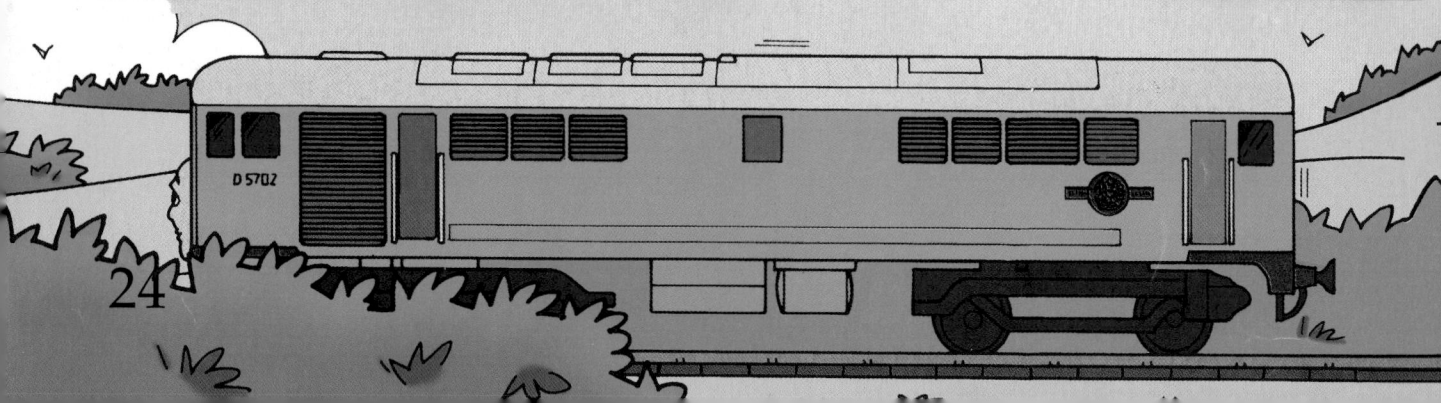

24

13. "Have you seen Bill and Ben?" their driver asks BoCo. "I want to put their name plates back on."

14. "Now I know what's going on!" says BoCo. "The twin engines played a trick on me! Ben pretended to be Bill, and Bill pretended to be Ben!"

15. BoCo plays a trick on THEM! When the twins say, "Hello, BoCo," he says, "I'm not BoCo. I'm CoBo, his twin." Bill and Ben are amazed!

16. Edward knows about BoCo's trick, and can't help laughing. And when he and BoCo explain the trick to Bill and Ben, they all enjoy the joke.

Double Trouble

Bill and Ben are twin engines, so it's difficult to tell who is who. These two pictures of them look the same, but there are five things that are different in the bottom picture. Can you find all five?

The answers are on page 61.

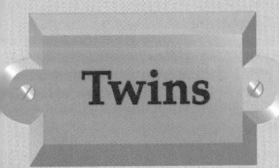

Twins

Donald and Douglas are twin engines. Draw a picture of Douglas in the empty frame at the bottom of the page. Copy the outline picture of Donald square by square, then colour the picture.

Donald

Douglas

Ten Trucks

Percy and Thomas are collecting trucks in the yard.
They are both happy little engines, and like to keep busy.
"I can collect ten trucks faster than you can!" says Thomas.
"No you can't!" says Percy. "I'm much faster!"

Who will be first to collect 10 trucks, Thomas or Percy?
Play this game with a friend to find out.
• You need a dice, a pencil and a counter each.
• Choose to be Thomas or Percy.
• Take turns to shake the dice. Move around the
yard from START the number of spaces you throw.
If you throw 3, move 3 spaces, and so on.
• Each time you land on a truck, draw a tick
in the score box. Keep going around the yard.
The first player to land on 10 trucks is the winner.

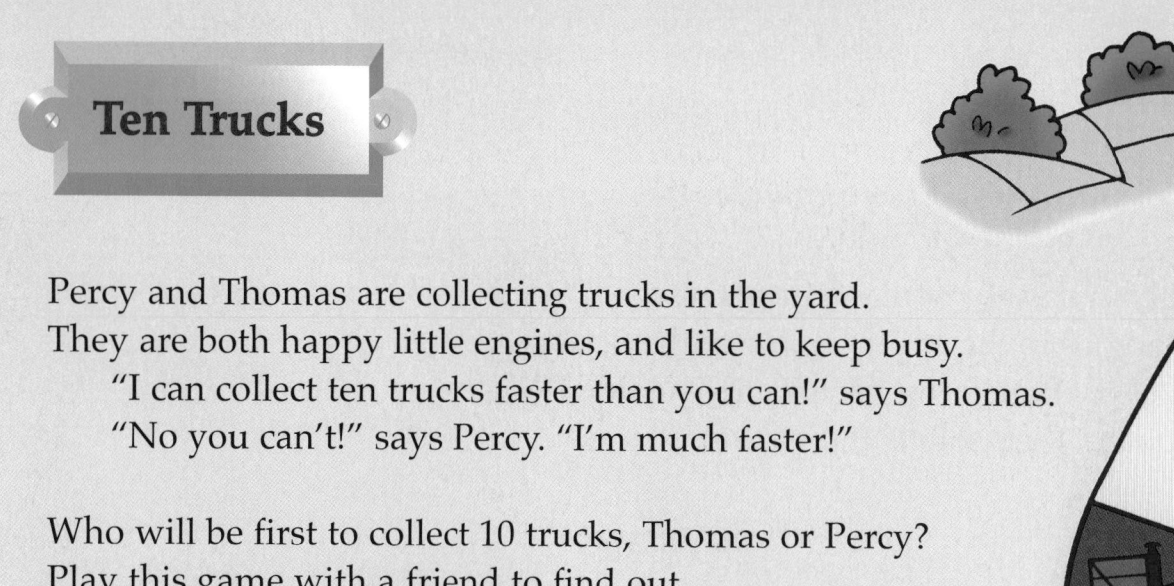

START

SCORE
Thomas' trucks

SCORE
Percy's trucks

Make a Thomas Bookmark

Bookmarks are very useful. When you are reading a book, they mark your place so that you know where you are up to. When you want to read again, you know which page to start from.

Make this Thomas bookmark and use it to keep your place.

You need:
a piece of white card
safety scissors
pencil
ruler
felt-tip pens

NOTE: always ask a grown-up to help you use scissors safely.

1. Measure and cut out a square of card 8cm wide and 8cm long.

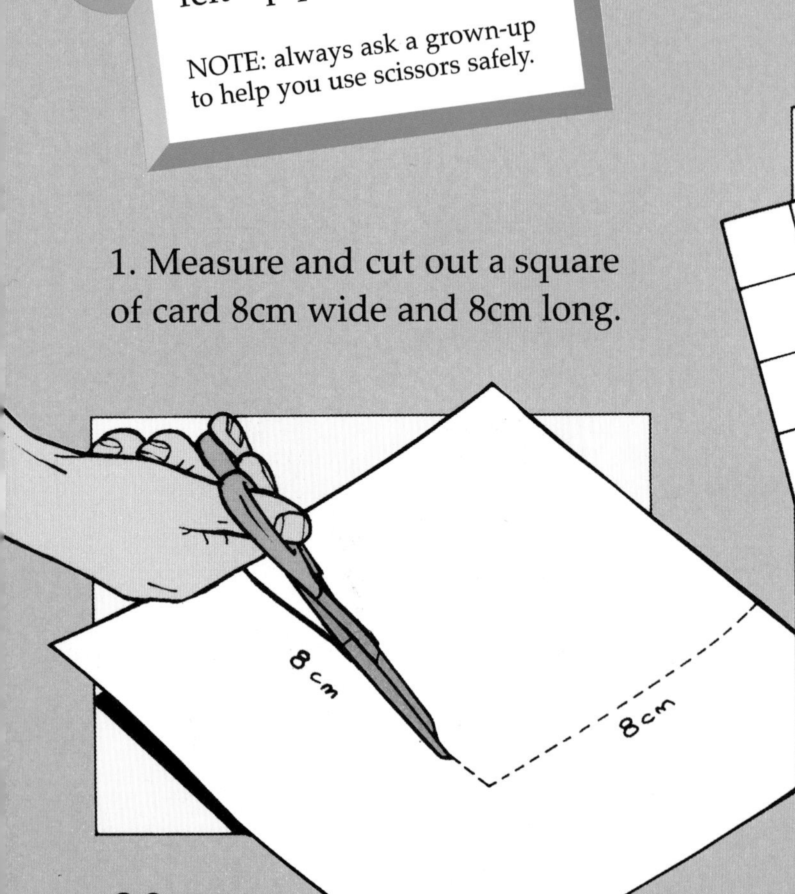

2. Measure and draw lines to divide the card into 16 squares, like this:

0.5 cm   0.5 cm

0.5 cm   0.5 cm

3. Draw the picture of Thomas. Copy it square by square.

4. Cut out the picture. Make two cuts,
one on each buffer, like this:

CUT

CUT OUT
SHAPE

CUT

5. Use felt-tip pens or coloured
pencils to colour the bookmark.
Colour the back, too.

6. Now your bookmark is ready to use. Slide
Thomas onto the page and let him keep your place.

Leaves on the Line

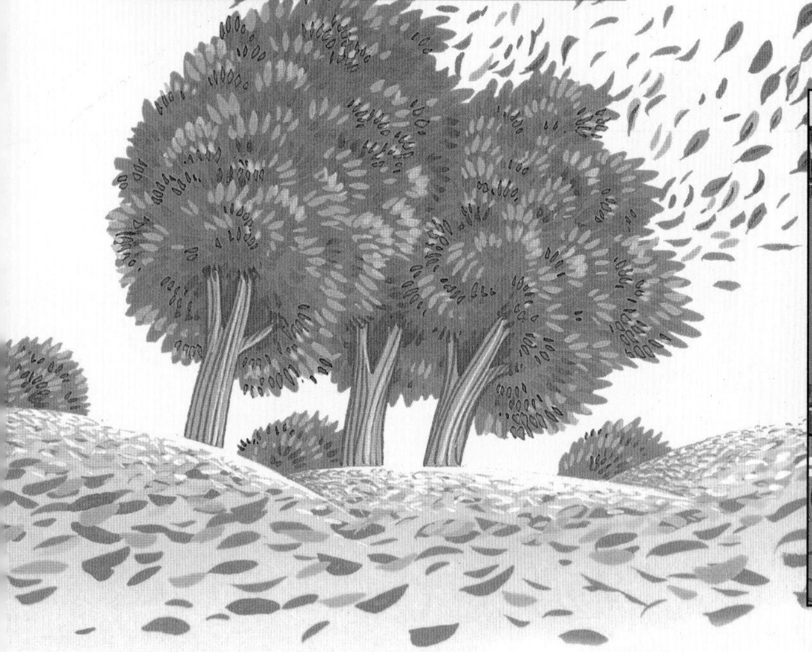

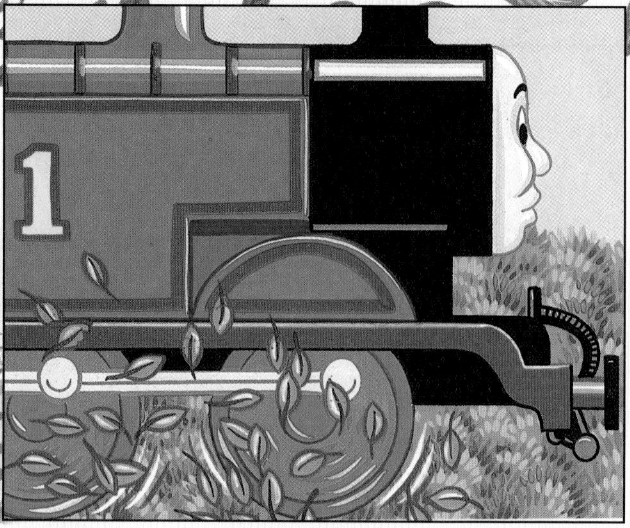

1. It is autumn on the Island of Sodor. The leaves on the trees are turning from green to brown and orange. They cover the ground like a carpet.

2. Thomas likes to see the autumn leaves. But he does not like it when rain makes them wet, because wet leaves make the rails very slippery.

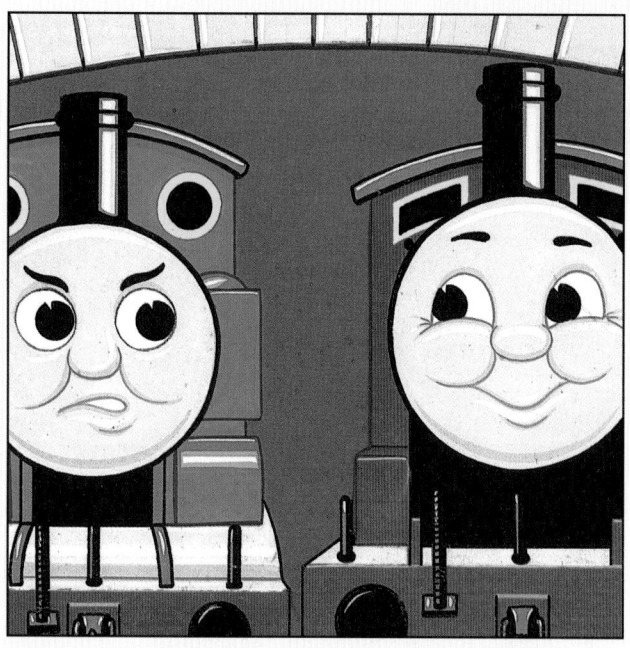

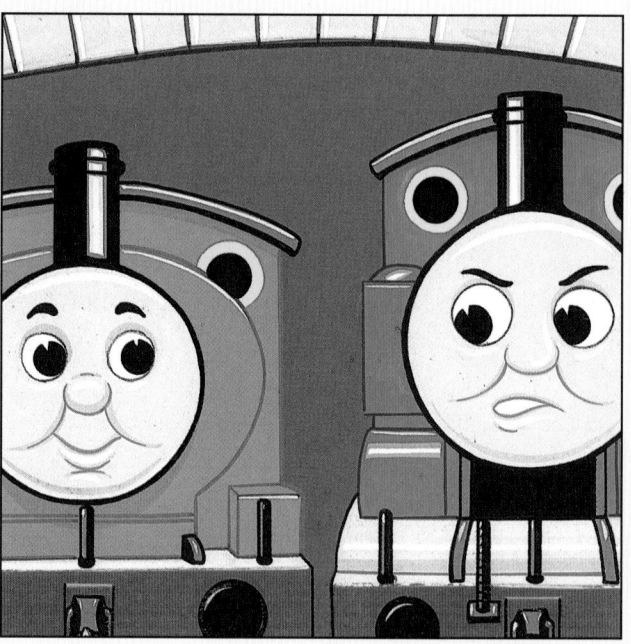

3. One night when Thomas comes into the shed James asks if he has had a good day. "No!" says Thomas. "Those wet leaves made the rails slippery!"

4. The next night is the same. "Did you have a good day, Thomas?" asks Percy. "No, I did not!" says Thomas. "Wet leaves on the line again!"

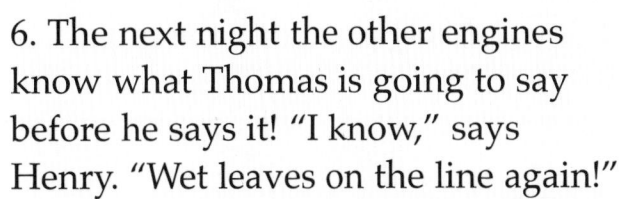

5. It rains and rains, and each night in the shed Thomas complains about the wet leaves making the rails slippery. He is a grumpy little engine!

6. The next night the other engines know what Thomas is going to say before he says it! "I know," says Henry. "Wet leaves on the line again!"

7. One morning Gordon has gone for the Express. Percy, Henry, Edward and James are still in the yard when Thomas speeds in, travelling backwards!

8. Thomas is in a real hurry and looks worried. "Leaves on the line again, Thomas?" asks Henry, and the other engines all start to laugh.

9. But Thomas doesn't find Henry's joke funny. "No, not leaves," says Thomas. "It's a TREE! The high winds have blown it down. It's lying across the rails!"

10. This is serious! A tree on the track is very dangerous. Thomas and his driver get the breakdown train and take it to the fallen tree as fast as they can.

11. The breakdown train tries to move the tree off the rails with cranes, but it will not budge. Terence the Tractor's big snow plough will not move it, either.

12. What can they do? In a few minutes Gordon is going to arrive with the Express train! Then Thomas has an idea. "This is job for Harold the Helicopter!" he says.

13. Thomas steams off, and gets back to the tree just as Harold flies over. Thomas' driver and fireman fix heavy chains from Harold to the tree.

14. Harold the Helicopter flies up slowly, higher and higher. The chains pull tight around the tree and soon it is lying at the side of the track, away from the rails.

15. Just in time! Thomas thanks Harold the Helicopter for his help and steams back to the Big Station. Gordon arrives a few minutes later with the Express.

16. That night in the shed Thomas tells Gordon all about the tree. "After today I promise I'll never complain about wet leaves on the line again!" he says.

Puffing Engines

Can you put the letters in the right order to spell the names of the engines?

1 **M A J E S**

2 **Y R H N E**

3 **R O G N O D**

4 WADRED

5 CKUD

6 YCREP

7 BOTY

8 HASOMT

37

18 Super Thomas the Tank Engine prizes to be won!

Would you like to have one of these great
Thomas the Tank Engine toys?
You may be lucky enough to win one if you enter this year's
Thomas the Tank Engine & Friends Annual competition!

All you have to do is to answer this question:

What colour is Henry and what number engine is he?

If you get the answer right, you might be the lucky winner of one of these prizes.
They are all made by Golden Bear.

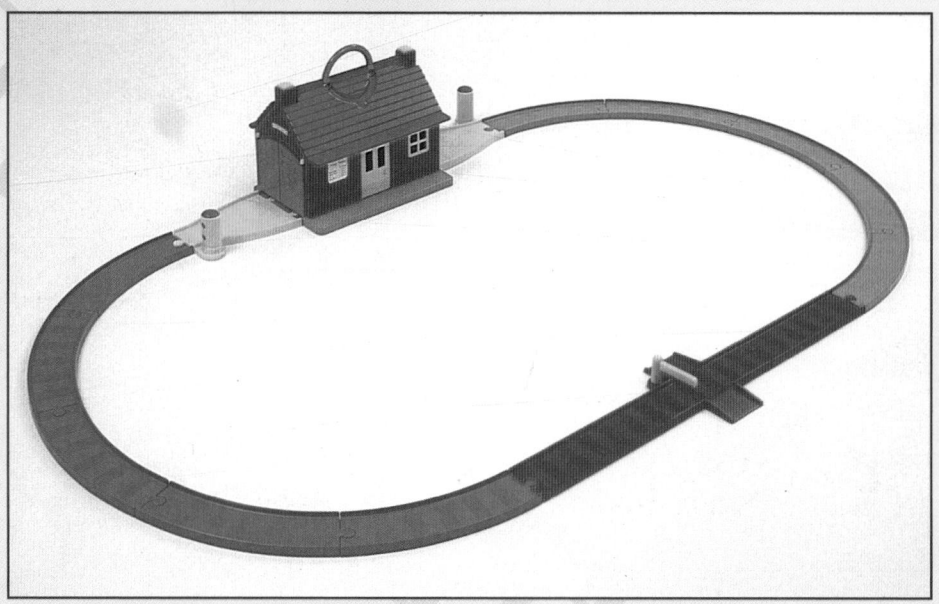

6 Thomas Station sets
containing an activity station,
level crossing and an oval track

6 Thomas Track sets
containing Thomas, Annie,
Clarabel and a circular track.

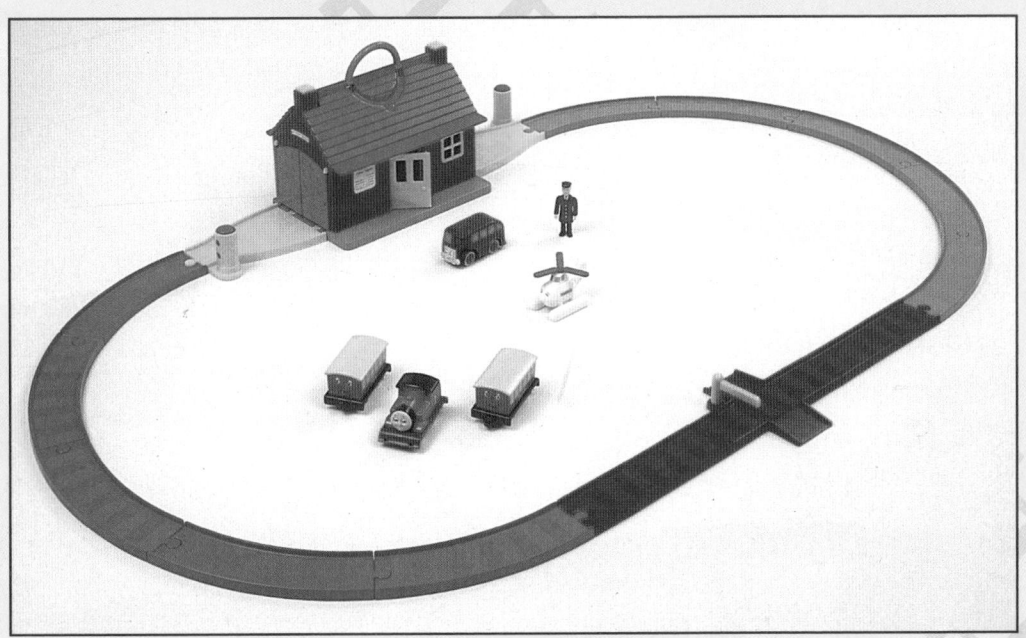

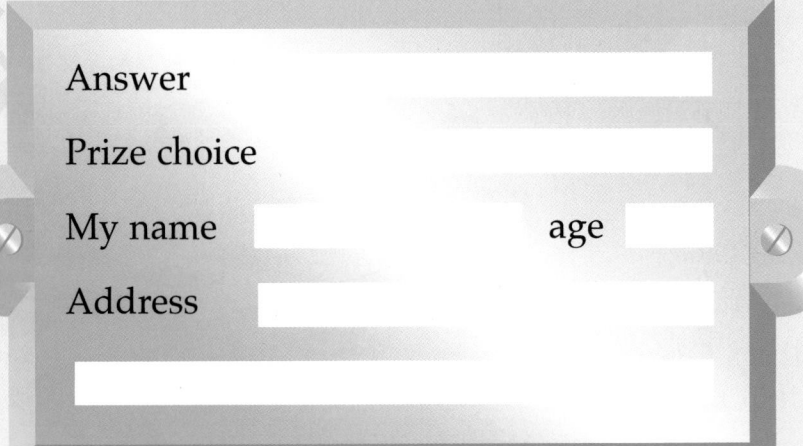

6 Thomas Deluxe sets containing Thomas, Annie, Clarabel, Harold, Bertie, the Station Master, a level crossing, activity station and an oval track.

Write your entry on a postcard, or on the back of a sealed envelope. There are three things you must remember to tells us:

Answer

Prize choice

My name   age

Address

1. Your **answer** to the question: Henry's name and number.

2. Which **prize** you would prefer: The **Thomas Station set**, **Thomas Track set** or **Thomas Deluxe set**.

3. Your **name, age** and **address**.

Send your entry to:
Thomas the Tank Engine & Friends Annual Competition, World International Limited,
Deanway Technology Centre, Wilmslow Road, Handforth, Cheshire, SK9 3FB.

The closing date is **Friday 15th January 1999**

RULES:
1. Eighteen winners will be chosen at random and notified by post.
2. Judges' decision will be final. No correspondence can be entered into.
3. A list of winners will be made available on request from World International Limited,
Deanway Technology Centre, Wilmslow Road, Handforth, Cheshire, SK9 3FB after February 14th 1999. Please enclose a s.a.e.
4. Employees (and their relatives) of World International Limited and their associated companies are not eligible to enter.
5. Entries are limited to one per person.
6. Competition is open to residents of the UK, Ireland and the Channel Islands.
7. The publishers reserve the right to vary the prizes, subject to availability.

Photographs courtesy of Golden Bear.

A Very Busy Day

The railway on Sodor is a very busy place. There's always something going on, and always jobs that need to be done. The engines and the staff are kept busy from morning till night.

7 o'clock
Henry goes to the harbour bright and early. The boats have come back with lots of fish, which have been loaded on to The Flying Kipper in boxes of ice. It's Henry's job to get the fish to the shops as soon as he can.

8 o'clock
Thomas is a cheerful, happy little engine who loves working on his own little branch line with his faithful coaches, Annie and Clarabel. They collect the men and take them to work at the quarry. Clarabel carries goods as well as passengers.

10 o'clock
Sir Topham Hatt, The Fat Controller, is in charge of the railway. It is his job to make sure that the engines and trains are neat and tidy for the passengers. He's always looking at his watch, because another of his important jobs is to make sure that the trains all run on time.

40

11 o'clock

"Eleven o'clock exactly," says Sir Topham Hatt. "Off you go, Gordon!" Gordon is the most powerful and the fastest of Sir Topham Hatt's engines. He always does the important job of pulling the Express passenger train.

12 o'clock

The yard is filling up with lots and lots of trucks that need keeping in order. "This is just the job for you, Percy!" Sir Topham Hatt tells the small junior engine. "Leave the trucks to me, Sir," says Percy, who is happy to puff around the yard all day. "I'll sort them out!"

1 o'clock

A coal truck has tipped its load of coal in the yard. It's a job for Donald and Douglas, the Scottish twin engines. They are hard workers, and because they're used to ploughing through snow, they'll soon clear the coal.

2 o'clock

The engines are always kept neat and tidy. Duck, whose real name is Montague, is a small tank engine. In a quiet part of the afternoon before the rush hour his driver washes his paint until it gleams. Duck still has the letters G W R on his side, which stand for Great Western Railway, from the time when he worked on the mainland.

4 o'clock

There are lots of China clay trucks in the yard that need sorting out. This is a job for Edward, one of the older engines. He's always kind, and never bumps the trucks. He's just the engine to put things in order, and soon the yard is neat and tidy again.

6 o'clock

Henry is a long, fast engine. He loves pulling the trains that bring passengers to the Big Station on their way home from work. He likes everything to be just right, so he's very pleased when he steams into the station and sees the Big Station clock that tells him he's right on time.

7 o'clock

Toby is a funny little tram engine with an odd shape. He's short and sturdy and works hard. Every night he has a very important job to do. He and his coach Henrietta take all the letters and parcels that have been posted on the island to meet up with the mail train.

8 o'clock

It's dark outside, and the engines have all done a hard day's work. Their drivers and firemen have gone home, and now it's time to rest. The engines settle down in the shed to talk about the day – and to look forward to another busy day tomorrow.

What a busy day the engines had! Write numbers and draw hour hands on the little clocks to show when things happened.

1. Henry goes to the harbour at __ o'clock.

2. Gordon sets off with the Express at __ o'clock.

3. Donald and Douglas clear coal at __ o'clock.

4. The engines go into their shed at __ o'clock.

The answers are on page 61.

Steam Power

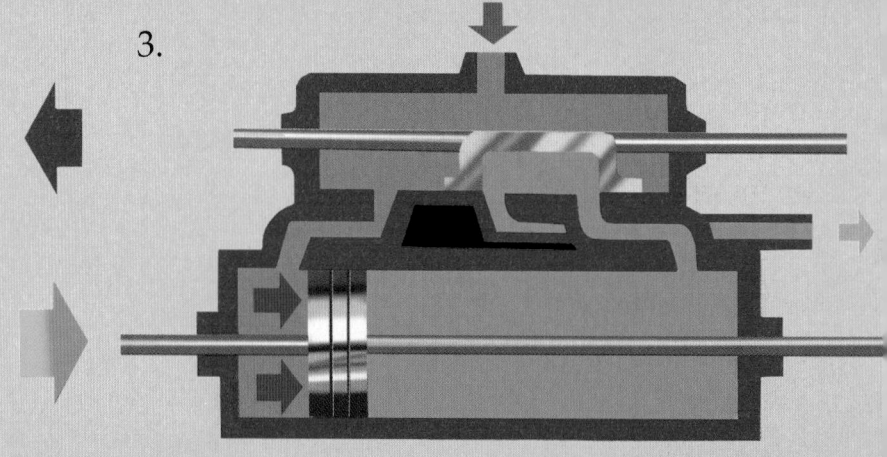

Engines are machines that change energy from fuel into movement.

Our bodies work like engines. Food is the fuel that gives our bodies the energy they need to move. Different kinds of food contain different amounts of energy.

Engines like Thomas are called steam engines. This is how they work.

1.
Coal is an engine's fuel (its 'food'). Coal is burned and makes hot gases.

2.
When the water boils it turns into steam. Steam is full of energy and takes up much more space than the water it came from.

3.
The steam expands (gets bigger and bigger) and pushes things called pistons, making them move.

1.

Steam in The hot gases go into a boiler and heat water.

2.

Steam out

The movement of the pistons turns the wheels that move the engine along.

3.

Percy's puzzle

The 6 pieces have all been taken from the big picture of Percy. Can you see where each piece has been taken from?

45

Toby Saves the Day

Thomas the Tank Engine and Toby the Tram Engine are very good friends. Toby and his coach, Henrietta, help Thomas to take workmen to the quarry every morning on Thomas' branch line. Toby also takes the mail to the big mail train each night.

One day Toby and Henrietta, and Thomas and his coaches, Annie and Clarabel, were coming back from the quarry and had to wait at a crossing until the signals changed before they could go on.

A smart new bus with lots of school children on board was at the crossing, too.

The bus driver leaned out of his open window and pointed to Toby. He started to laugh. "Look at that funny old thing!" said the driver. "It's like a shed on wheels! And just look at that coach. It was going to be used as a hen house before it was brought here, you know!" He turned around and spoke to the children on the bus. "That engine is what was used to take people around before fine buses like this one came along!" he said. "What a mess! I'd rather have this smart new bus any day!"

Toby likes to blow his whistle to say hello, but he felt too cross and upset to do it that day.

Thomas didn't. "Peep, PEEP!" he said angrily. The bus driver was very rude! Thomas didn't think he should laugh at Toby like that. Toby is a funny shape, it's true, but he's very useful, and a really hard worker. Thomas didn't like him being made fun of.

Thomas was glad when the bus drove off, and so was Toby.

After a busy morning, Thomas saw the bus again. It was sitting by the side of the railway track, and it was leaning to one side a bit. Thomas soon saw why. One of its wheels had come off!

The children waved to Thomas and his driver put on the brakes. Thomas' driver asked if he could help.

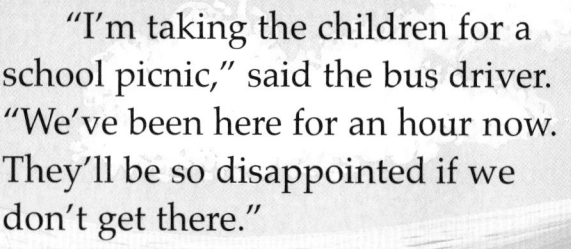

"I'm taking the children for a school picnic," said the bus driver. "We've been here for an hour now. They'll be so disappointed if we don't get there."

"We'll try to help," said Thomas' driver. "My engine, Thomas, is busy this afternoon, but Toby will be able to help you. He has some spare time before he has to collect the post."

Thomas and his driver hurried off, and were soon back with Toby and Henrietta.

The children all got off the bus and on to Henrietta. Their big picnic baskets fitted on, too, and they set off. Some of the children had never been on a train before, and they loved the clackety-clack sound the wheels made on the rails. They had a lovely view of the countryside through Henrietta's big windows. They all enjoyed the ride Toby gave them, and squealed with delight when he blew his whistle extra loud.

"Do it again, Toby!" they cried.
"Do it again, please!"

Soon the children were enjoying
their picnic in a big meadow filled
with wild flowers. They spread out
their food under a shady tree and
played games. Toby and Henrietta
waited quietly in a little siding.

At the end of the afternoon the
smart new bus arrived to take the
children back to school. Thomas'
driver had sent some mechanics
to mend the broken wheel.

"Here we are at last!" called the
driver. "All aboard for the journey
home! You'll be pleased to know
that you don't have to go back
on that funny old engine."

49

But there was a big surprise for the bus driver. The children didn't want to go back to school on his bus – they told their teachers that they liked Toby and Henrietta much more than the shiny new bus. They liked the way the coach swayed from side to side, and the noises the wheels made on the track. Best of all they liked the way Toby blew his whistle extra loud for them. They had enjoyed their journey so much that they wanted to go back on the train.

Toby and Henrietta still had some time to spare, and they were pleased to be able to take the children back again.

The children pointed to the new bus as it drove along beside the railway track – empty. The bus driver didn't look very pleased with himself now.

The bus picked up the children at the little station, but the driver had to wait until the children had all said a special thank you and goodbye.

The children patted and stroked Toby and Henrietta's smooth sides. "Thank you for the lovely ride," they said. "You're a lovely engine, Toby, and we don't think you're funny or old fashioned at all. We like you, and you made the picnic extra special."

Toby was so
pleased that he blew
them an extra loud whistle.
When the children were on
the bus they waved and waved
until they were out of sight.
Toby and Henrietta were still at the
station when Thomas came along. "Well done,
Toby. You saved the children's picnic and gave
them a nice ride," said Thomas. "You're more
useful than a shiny new bus any day!"

51

"Here are some pictures from the story of Toby and
Henrietta. There are some words and names too.
Can you read the words, then write each on the line
near its picture? You ARE clever! Peep, peep!"

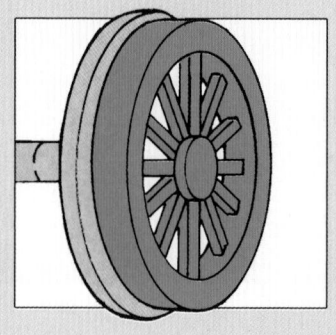

_____

_____

_____

_____

_____

_____

_____

_____

_____

bus	wheel	Thomas	tree
Toby	flowers	Henrietta	picnic driver

52

Count with Thomas

There is a lot going on at the Big Station today.
There are lots of things to see and do.

Look at the little pictures and count
how many you can see in the picture.
Write a number in each little wheel shape.

The answers are on page 61.

Thomas around the world

1 USA

Thomas the Tank Engine appears at the National Railroad Museum, Wisconsin, at a 'Friends of Thomas' event. Thomas appears to audiences in America in his own show entitled 'Shining Time Station', where he is introduced to viewers by Mr Conductor, a magical figure only seen by children, who lives in a mural on the wall of the railway station.

3 UK

Owners of VHE Construction near Barnsley turn one of their diesel storage tanks into a cheerful Christmas attraction. At night, when Thomas is lit up, it looks as though his wheels are moving!

2 AUSTRALIA

Thomas leaves his tracks behind for a ride along the sea front in Glenelg, near Adelaide, Australia. This gentleman scoops first prize in this annual competition, with a sand-sculpture of Thomas.

54

UK

The biggest Thomas ever takes to the skies for an early-morning view of London.

The hot air balloon's vital statistics are:

Overall length 28.8 m
Width 11.4 m
Height 20.1 m
Gauge 7.2 m (five times larger than standard railway gauge)

Previous to this launch at Tower Bridge, it was installed near the entrance to the Nurenburg Toy Fair in Germany to highlight the presence of Thomas TV and product.

5 JAPAN

Thomas the Tank snow-sculptures at the 47th Sapporo Snow Festival, February 1996, complete with snow-slides!

4 NEW ZEALAND

While Thomas is in Australia, some of his friends visit the Glenbrook Vintage Railway in New Zealand.

55

Blowing Bubbles

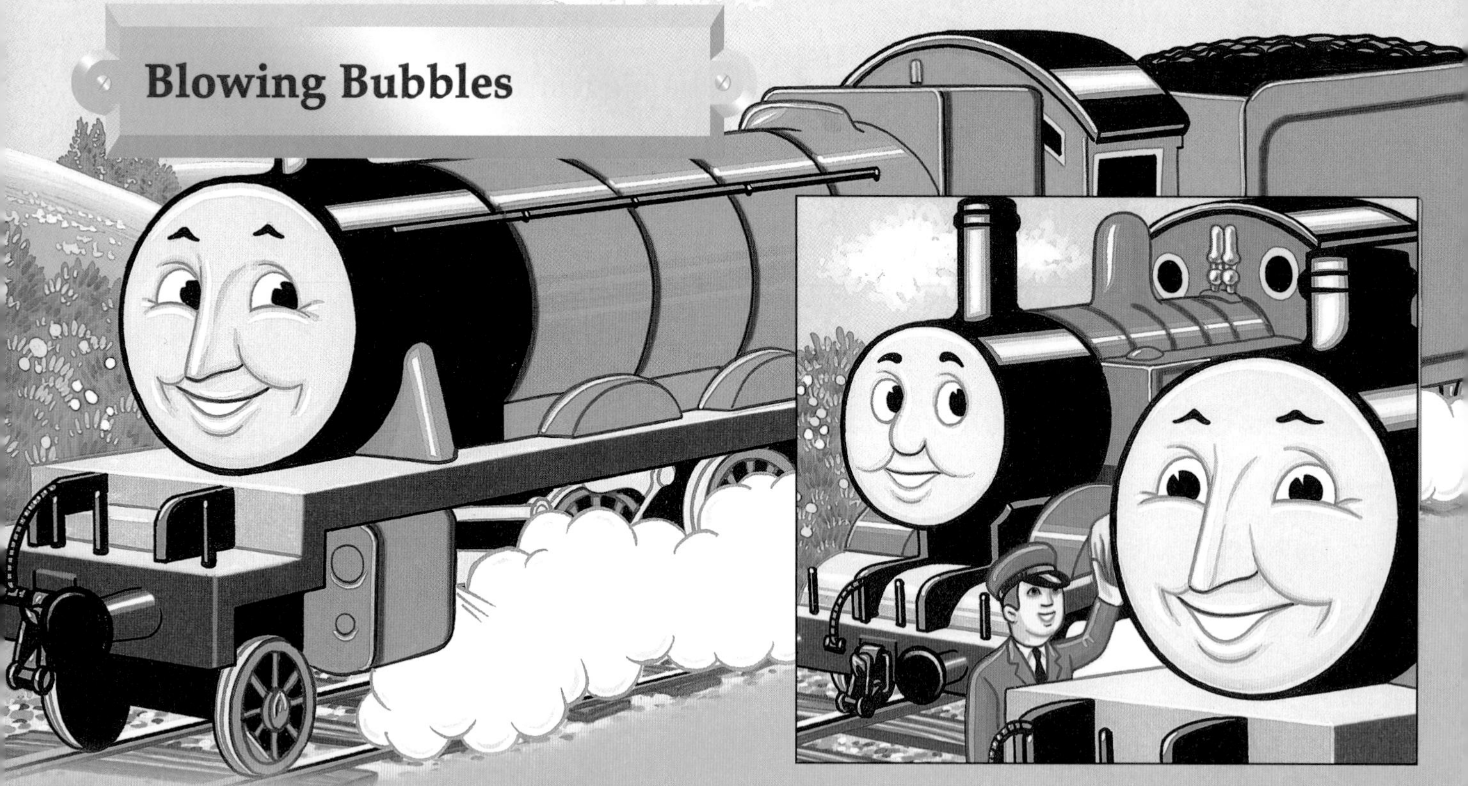

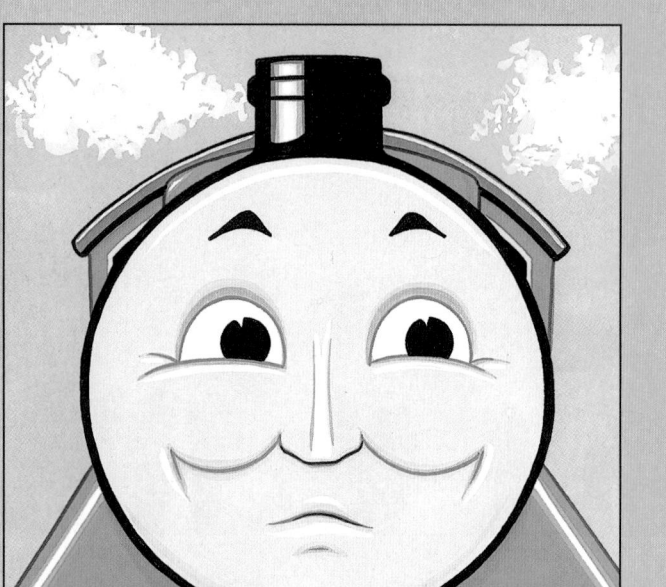

1. Henry is very proud indeed of his shiny green paint. He doesn't like going out in the rain in case he gets it wet and dirty.

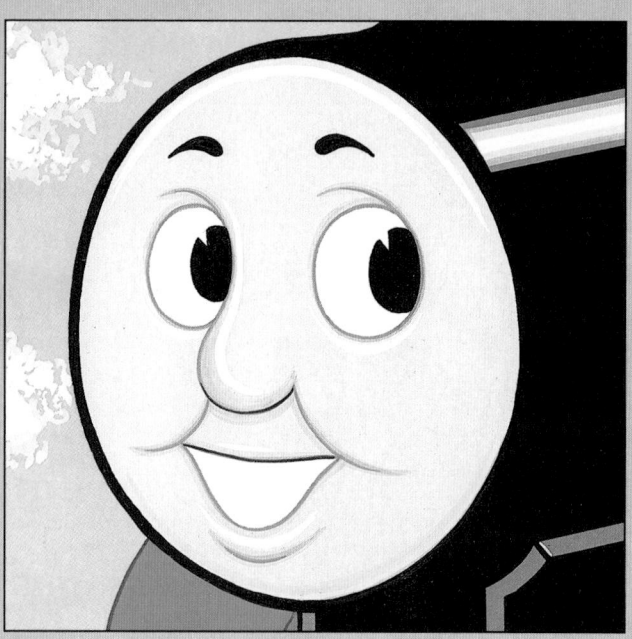

2. One day his driver is washing Henry when cheeky little Thomas chuffs by. "Come on, Slow-coach!" says Thomas. "You'll be late if you don't hurry."

3. Henry looks very puzzled. He has no idea what Thomas is talking about. "Late for what, Thomas?" he asks. "Oh, and don't call me Slow-coach!"

4. Thomas laughs. "All right, Fast-coach!" But you have forgotten, haven't you? It's the Open Day at the Big Station today. The children are waiting for us!"

5. Thomas is right. Henry HAS forgotten. But he has been looking forward to the chance to show himself off at the Open Day and is anxious to be off.

6. Henry's driver doesn't have time to finish rinsing the soap suds off Henry. But Henry doesn't care for once – he can't wait to get to the Big Station.

7. Henry is the last engine to arrive, and gets to the Big Station puffing and blowing. There's a big crowd of children watching from the platform.

8. Henry steams to a stop just as Sir Topham Hatt, The Fat Controller, says, "Please welcome number 3, Henry, our fast green engine!"

9. The children all cheer and clap. "Oh, isn't he a fine engine?" says one girl. "Yes, just look at his shiny green paint!" says another. "He's so smart!"

10. Henry is really delighted! He is so pleased and happy to hear the children saying such nice things about him!

11. "Say hello, Henry!" says Sir Topham Hatt. Henry doesn't need telling twice, and he decides to celebrate and say "Peep, peep!" at the same time.

12. Henry takes a deep, deep breath, and blows lots of steam out of his funnel as hard as he can. The children always enjoy that – and so does Henry!

13. But what a surprise! Instead of steam, hundreds and hundreds of tiny, shiny soap bubbles float from his funnel. The Big Station is full of them!

14. The children clap and cheer as the bubbles float around them. "Henry isn't just a handsome engine," says one little boy. "He's clever as well."

15. Henry feels more pleased than ever and blows even more soap bubbles out of his funnel. The children have lots of fun trying to catch them.

16. An extra big bubble lands on top of Sir Topham Hatt's hat. But he doesn't mind. The Open Day is a great success, thanks to Henry and his bubbles!

Bubbles

The children were pleased when Henry blew lots and lots of soap
bubbles out of his funnel. How many bubbles can you count and colour?

Answers to Puzzles

Famous Engines (page 19)

1. Rocket
2. Locomotion
3. Big Boy
4. English
5. Stourbridge Lion

Which Way? (page 21)

Edward should go along track D.

Double Trouble (page 26)

Puffing Engines (page 36)

1. JAMES
2. HENRY
3. GORDON
4. EDWARD
5. DUCK
6. PERCY
7. TOBY
8. THOMAS

A Very Busy Day (page 43)

1. 7 o'clock
2. 11 o'clock
3. 1 o'clock
4. 8 o'clock

Percy's Puzzle (page 45)

Count with Thomas (page 53)

There are :
4 fish boxes
1 clock
5 mail sacks
2 seats
3 posters

Bubbles (page 60)

There are 15 bubbles.